The Egyptian Polar Bear

JoAnn Adinolfi

Houghton Mifflin Company
Boston 1994

My first book was made possible through a special
grant of love and support from my Mother and Father.
Thanks Mom! Thanks Dad!

Grazie tante!
Donna, James, Jeanne Berg, Barbara Bartolomeo
and Deborah Kogan Ray.

DANKESCHÖN KARSTEN!

Library of Congress Cataloging-in-Publication Data

Adinolfi, JoAnn.
   The Egyptian polar bear / written and illustrated by JoAnn
Adinolfi.
      p.   cm.
   Summary: A lonely polar bear is swept away on an iceberg and winds
up in Egypt where he becomes the royal playmate of Rahotep the boy
king.
   ISBN 0-395-68074-3
   [1. Polar bear—Fiction.   2. Bears—Fiction.   3. Egypt—Fiction.]
      I. Title.
PZ7. A26115Eg   1994   93-34050
[E]—dc20   CIP
                               AC

Printed in the United States of America

WOZ   10   9   8   7   6   5   4   3   2   1

According to historians,
the hieroglyphics from an ancient tomb
record an architect's plans for
a burial vault for a polar bear.
How this bear got to Egypt has never
been discovered and barely guessed at.

Way up north in the icy Arctic lived Nanook the polar bear. He liked playing in the snow, swimming in the cold sea, and hunting seals, but he was often very lonely.

One day Nanook climbed atop a
huge iceberg to see if he could spot
a fellow bear to play with. Suddenly a
strong current swept the iceberg out to
the open sea, starting Nanook south
on an unexpected journey.

Nanook soon sailed past the British Isles. He took a turn at Spain, squeezed by the Rock of Gibraltar into the warm waters of the Mediterranean Sea, and rounded the boot of Italy. Throughout the long journey, the iceberg grew smaller and smaller until it melted into a tiny ice cube which was much too little for Nanook.

Nanook sank into the warm sea and swam toward land.
He landed exhausted on the sandy shores of Egypt. The broiling
sun beat down on him. He had never felt such heat. He could
see nothing he recognized and realized that he was far, far from
home. Hungry and thirsty, he fell asleep on the unfamiliar shore.

When Nanook awoke, he found himself surrounded by amazed Egyptian sailors. They had never seen a polar bear before. The sailors decided Nanook must have been sent by the gods and that he should be taken straight to Rahotep the boy king. Nanook went willingly, for he was too hungry and weak to fight. He boarded a boat which sailed along the Nile River to Thebes, where King Rahotep's palace stood.

Rahotep the boy king was only ten years old. Though he was the powerful, rich king of Egypt, he had no friends and was very lonely. He didn't laugh, he never said please, and he rarely said thank you.

Rahotep was taking a nap on his throne when the palace doors flew open with a bang. Rahotep sat up straight and rubbed his sleepy eyes. He wanted to look regal and brave but he was afraid of the great white bear in his doorway.

He stepped down from his throne and walked very slowly toward Nanook. He shook so much he could hardly keep his balance.

Nanook also was frightened, and he let out a thunderous roar. Rahotep tried to look brave. He spoke to Nanook with the voice of a king, not a boy. He said, "On behalf of the sun god Ré, I command you to be still." Nanook stood up on his hind legs. The king's court gasped. "Silence!" shouted Rahotep. "I command you, beast, to sit!" Nanook bared his teeth. He was scared of Rahotep.

Rahotep thought for a moment. He clapped his hands and summoned the carriers of cool drinks, the preparers of sweets, and the minister of meat to bring a feast. "Be quick!" he cried. "The beast is hungry and thirsty!"

When the feast was ready, King
Rahotep offered the great bear a juicy
piece of goose. Nanook sniffed at the
meat. He knew it wasn't seal. Rahotep
leaned over and whispered in
Nanook's ear, "Please, eat." Nanook
slowly opened his mouth. Everyone
held their breath. Rahotep could see
each one of the bear's very large teeth.
He stood firm and waited. Finally,
Nanook ate the piece of goose from
the king's hand.

Rahotep sighed. The court applauded the king's bravery. Nanook ate until his belly was full. Rahotep felt proud that he had tamed the beast. Nanook was happy because he was no longer hungry and thirsty, and he felt Rahotep was a friend he could trust.

That night, Nanook let Rahotep pet him. He felt the warmth of the boy king's hand upon him and fell asleep. Rahotep curled up against Nanook and forgot about being king and being unhappy. "Tomorrow I shall play all day," he thought.

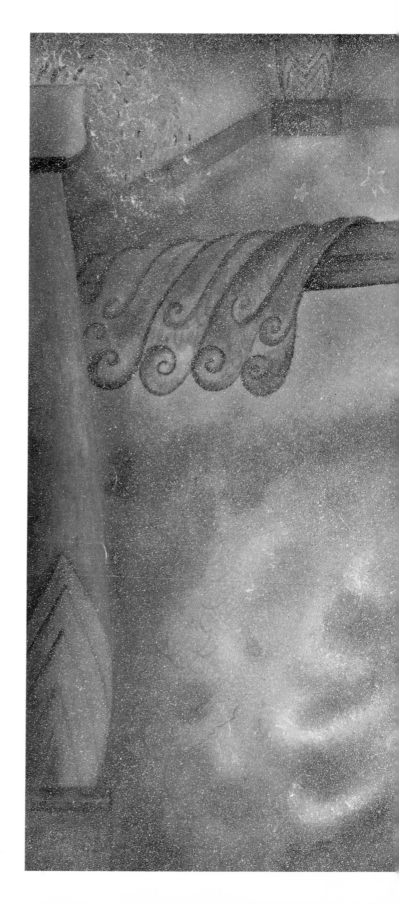

Rahotep and Nanook rose early the next morning, eager to start their day. After a big breakfast, they took a bath in the royal tub. It was the first time Nanook felt cool since he had arrived in Egypt, and it was the first time ever that Rahotep had fun taking a bath. He scrubbed behind Nanook's ears and made sure that the black pads under his paws were all clean. After their bath, they both smelled of flowery perfume. Rahotep declared the royal bath Nanook's room so Nanook would be free to cool off whenever the weather became too hot for him.

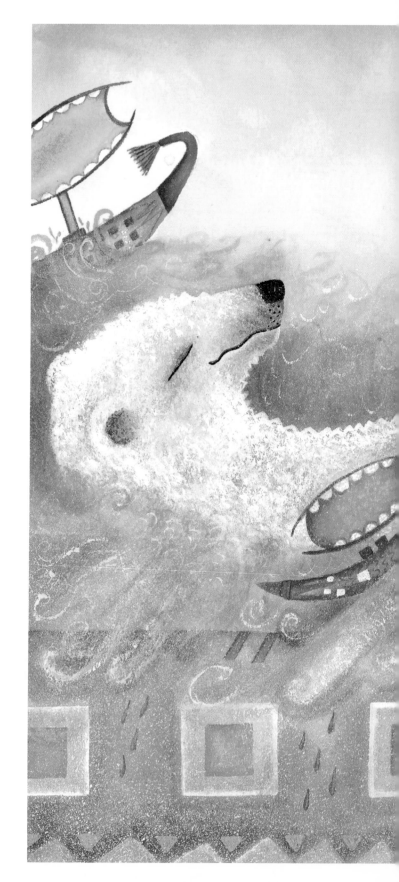

Rahotep dressed Nanook in a gold and lapis lazuli collar with a grand medallion and officially presented him to the Royal Court. "I, King Rahotep," he said, "declare Nanook, the great white bear, the Royal Playmate of the king. Today there will be no work," he gladly said. "My friend and I are going to play."

First Rahotep gave Nanook a tour of the palace so he would know his way around. Nanook was so big and clumsy that he knocked over many valuable vases and statues of gods. This made the boy king laugh as never before.

Since it was a bit too small and crowded in the palace, Rahotep took Nanook outside to play. Nanook had more fun that day than he had ever had in the Arctic. It was great to be the king's Royal Playmate! He went hunting for exotic beasts like the sphinx and the griffin. He learned how to dance and got the hang of all the latest steps.

Nanook and Rahotep took a ride to the great temple in
a sedan chair which had to be carried by a hundred men.
They went swimming in the Nile, ate heaps of food, and
were fanned whenever they got too warm.

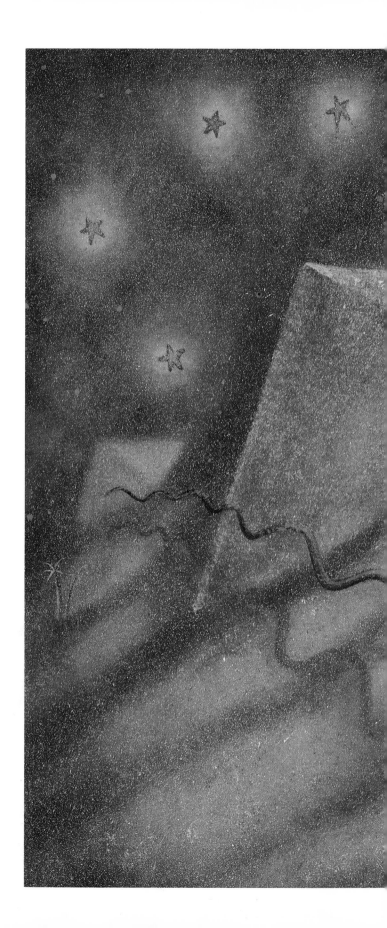

Everything was fine until that evening, when Nanook became homesick. He wished that the pyramids were icebergs and that the sand was snow. Rahotep saw that Nanook was unhappy and decided to take him pyramid climbing to cheer him up. The two friends reached the top of a huge pyramid and gazed at the stars.

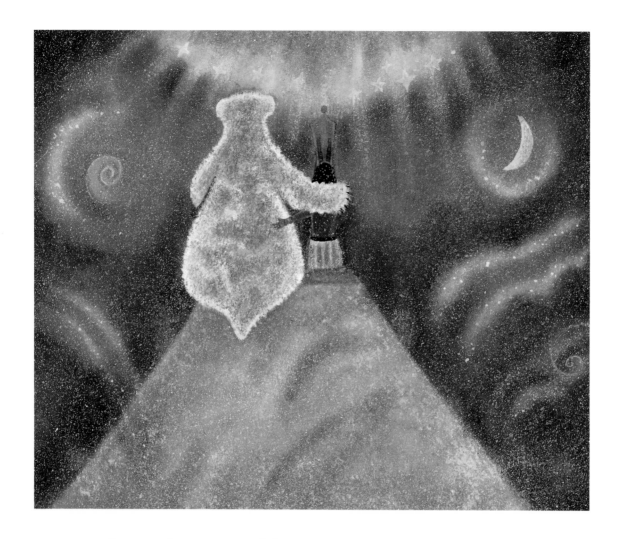

Nanook saw that some of the stars looked the same in Egypt as they did in the Arctic, and for the first time he felt at home. He felt safe with Rahotep at his side and the familiar sky above him.

Nanook and the young king sat at the top of the great pyramid until the sun rose. They were now inseparable friends. Nanook was truly an Egyptian polar bear, and Rahotep was the happiest, kindest king—although he never did learn to say please to everyone. He said please only to Nanook.